The HIPPO that FLEW

Zev Lewinson

Illustrations by Peter Cooper

SwordPen.com, Inc.
www.swordpen.com
SwordPen Publishers

Library of Congress Number:
2008932598
Lewinson, Zev

The Hippo That Flew / Zev Lewinson 1st ed.
Summary: Wilbur the hippo endlessly devotes his entire life's work
in the pursuit of flight for all hippo-mankind. His efforts finally
pay off in a most unusual way – and forever!

ISBN-13: 978-0-9799653-4-0
ISBN-10: 0-9799653-4-9

First Edition 2010 / Illustrated by Debi Coules
Edited by Caryn Starr, Avrahom Lewinson, and Gramlee.com
Jacket design and layout by www.rosettecreative.com

Printed in the USA

Dedicated to
the spirit that soars
within us all.

Once upon a time, there was a young hippopotamus named Wilbur. Wilbur had large blue eyes—as blue as the sky where he wished he could fly. In fact, Wilbur was sure that one day, he actually **would fly.**

"I'm flying!"

he would shout with delight, as he ran with his arms outstretched. In his make-believe world, he was a soaring eagle, swooping and swirling and somersaulting in the sky.

"Hippos don't fly," his friends and family would scold him. But Wilbur, the soon-to-be-flying hippo, refused to believe them. "Well, *I* can," he confidently proclaimed. "Give me a little time and you'll see … I will fly one of these days—for real!"

Everyone who saw him said, "Hippos are fat and heavy. They are the last creatures on the planet that could ever fly!"

"You are a crazy hippo," his peers said mockingly. As he grew older, even his teachers told him to forget his dream. "Enough with your childhood fantasies, Wilbur," they scolded. "Hippos do not—and will not ever—fly!"

But Wilbur insisted that he could fly,
and fly he would! He was determined, and

nothing would stop him,

especially not a little problem like gravity!

And so he spent hours and hours, and days
and weeks, observing all the different birds
in the sky and what it was that made them fly.
He gazed at the eagles as they soared, and
stared at the hummingbirds as they hovered.

Then one day, an idea popped into his head …

"I'll make my own wings!"

Wilbur decided.

Wilbur waxed a ton of feathers together and shaped them into enormous wings, because he read that feathers are what carry a bird in flight.

"If I attach enough feathers to carry even *my* weight, I will be able to fly," he reasoned.

Once Wilbur finished the wings, he climbed up to
the top of a mountain. He strapped on the wings,
ran to the edge of the cliff and jumped off.

Wilbur began to soar!

"Oh, what fun!"

he screeched in excitement. But soon the hot sun
melted the wax, the feathers fluttered apart, and
Wilbur fell to the ground. Luckily for Wilbur, he
didn't crash-land, because he landed on his bottom.
And hippos have very big, cushiony bottoms.

"Why don't you just give up?" the other hippos asked.
They laughed as they pointed at his big, slightly bruised bottom.
But Wilbur refused to give in.

"I WILL Fly!"
he said, as he totally ignored the negativity
and rude taunts of his peers.

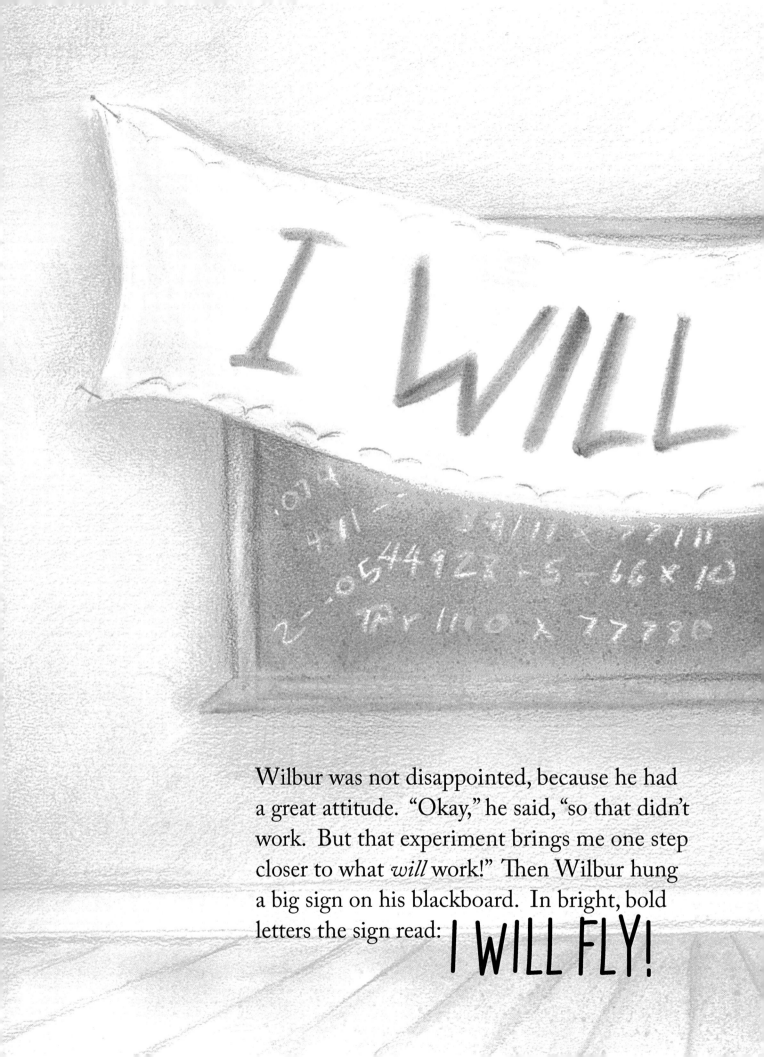

Wilbur was not disappointed, because he had a great attitude. "Okay," he said, "so that didn't work. But that experiment brings me one step closer to what *will* work!" Then Wilbur hung a big sign on his blackboard. In bright, bold letters the sign read: **I WILL FLY!**

FLY

I will FLY
I WILL FLY
I WILL FLY
I WILL FLY

Wilbur drew lots of little wings around the border of the sign and got back to work on his greatest passion.

Wilbur's family and friends got back to work, too—giving Wilbur what they felt was great advice.

"Give up! Hippos can't fly," said his classmates in the schoolyard. "Get a real job, son," his father advised. "And with good benefits," he added.

I WILL

"You're too fat to fly!" his younger brother Orville teased. "Get real!" his sister sneered.

"Please get your head out of the clouds, my son," his spiritual guide, the Holy Hippo, gently persuaded. "Flying is very dangerous, Wilbur!" his mother pleaded.

But Wilbur merely smiled and boldly stated his new motto,

"I WILL FLY!"

"I'll be careful, Mom," he promised, "but I WILL FLY! It is my dream! And it means everything in the world to me!"

"I WILL FLY," he kept repeating to himself confidently. After all, Wilbur didn't just wish he could fly. He didn't just hope he could fly. Wilbur knew for certain that one day he was *going* to fly! And no one—absolutely no one—was going to stop him. "I WILL FLY. I WILL FLY. **I WILLBUR FLY!"**

His goal was now crystal clear—as clear as the bluest sky on the very sunniest of days. And so Wilbur continued to observe the birds in the sky. He studied mountains of books about flying and voraciously read anything having to do with the science of aerodynamics. Wilbur no longer even heard the taunts, doubts, and disbelief of those around him.

Wilbur grew up and met a beautiful hippo named Beverly, and it was **love at first flight.**

He felt as if he were flying just by looking at her! Before long, they married and soon had three cute little baby hippos.

But even with a beautiful family to
keep him busy, Wilbur still constantly
daydreamed about flying.

His mind soared

and ideas floated around in his head about
all the possible ways that a hippo might
get himself off the ground.

As Wilbur grew older, he grew more determined than ever—especially as he gazed into the mirror at his graying beard— to discover a way to fly.

As a matter of fact, Wilbur was very fond of saying "time flies," having invented the famous expression!

Wilbur experimented with rockets and gliders, and calculated all possible mathematical equations to get himself off the ground. He kept notes on everything he did and wrote textbooks about his experiments.

And so the seasons passed, and time flew faster than even Wilbur ever imagined it could. Wilbur was now a very old hippo. He spent a lot of time in his rocking chair on the porch, holding the hand of his "navigator" (as he'd lovingly nicknamed Beverly), while gazing longingly at the sky.

Wilbur would murmur, "I WILL FLY! I WILL FLY! I WILLBUR FLY!"

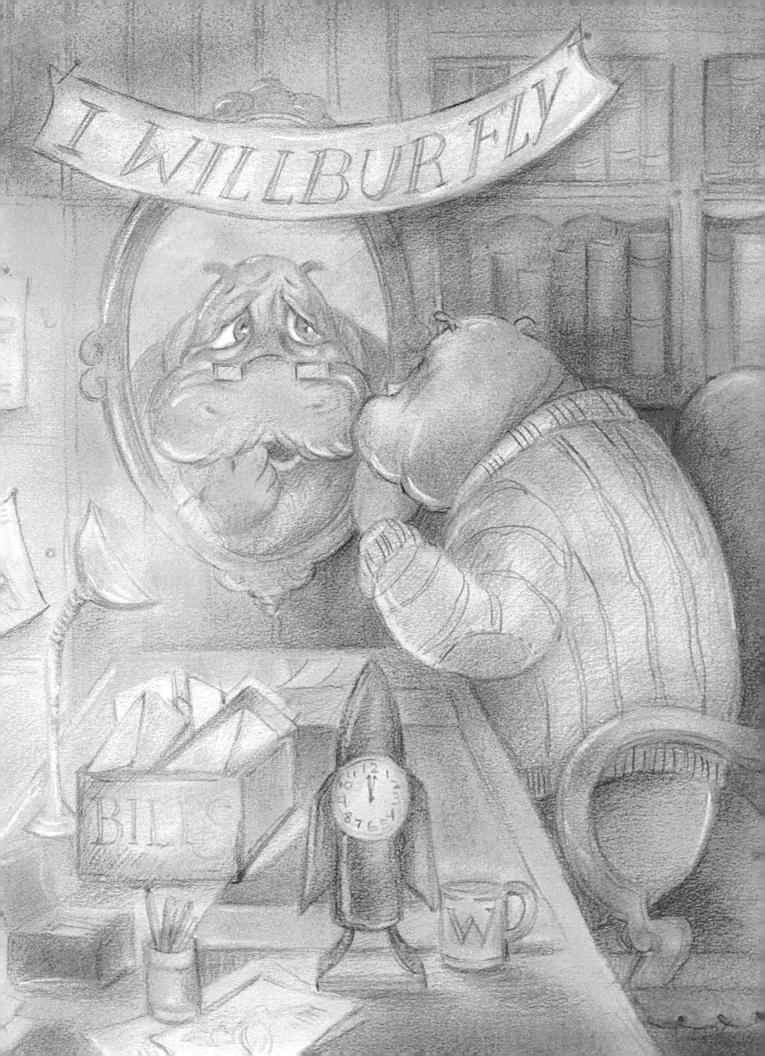

Sometimes he would rock very fast in his chair, as if to take off.
His wife and children watched in great sadness. "Poor Dad,"
his daughter said. "He can barely even walk, let alone fly."

Shortly thereafter, time finally stood still for Wilbur.
He passed from this world into the next with his

dream for flight still unfulfilled.

Wilbur's loved ones cherished his memory, but
felt sad that he had never achieved his life's most
passionate goal.

The Holy Hippo talked fondly about Wilbur among his family and friends. They all remembered his childhood fantasies, and could picture Wilbur with his arms outstretched, making believe that he was an eagle soaring through the air.

Then the Holy Hippo said a very powerful thing. "Of one thing I am certain," he said haltingly, **"Wilbur now has wings."**

Those who loved Wilbur nodded and felt full of happiness.

Little did anyone on Earth realize how true those words were. For as the last respects were spoken, and as his loved ones sighed, Wilbur floated up towards heaven.

A great Voice greeted him and said, "Welcome Wilbur, and congratulations!"

"Why are you congratulating me?" asked Wilbur.
"I never succeeded in my quest for flight."

"Ah, but you *did* succeed, Wilbur,"

said The Voice. "You have become an inspiration to all those on Earth who will follow after you. You held onto your belief in spite of what others said. You believed in yourself and your dreams, and used your Wilbur willpower as much as—forgive the insult—humanly possible."

"But still … I never flew," said Wilbur hesitatingly.

The Voice responded wisely. "But Wilbur, your children and other great individuals will use all the textbooks and notes you wrote and left behind, and they will pick up where you left off.

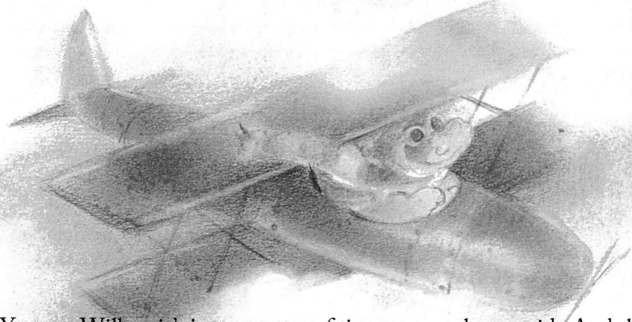

You see, Wilbur, it's just a matter of time, as you always said. And the one thing we have plenty of up here … is time!"

"Flight will happen down on Earth, Wilbur," The Voice continued. "It will happen because of your vision and determination. And you are the true inventor of it all," The Voice gently proclaimed.

Wilbur began to understand what The Voice was telling him! He was so excited that he almost didn't notice the tingling sensations in his fingers and toes, and his massive body suddenly felt

as light as air.

"The ability to fly was always there in your mind, Wilbur," The Voice told him. "One lifetime was simply not enough to sort out all the details. But you are hereby recognized and commended as The Creator of Flight on Earth," said The Voice.

"You now have the one thing you've always wanted ever since you were just a little boy, Wilbur," The Voice lovingly informed him.

"Fly, my son!"

Wilbur merely had to think about flying and he was able to take off—vertically, horizontally, or like a rocket! He could even hover.

"This is so cool!" Wilbur cried out in pleasure and joy as he tested his newfound power.

"Your powers of flight will only be limited by your imagination," The Voice explained.

"Thank you! Thank you! Thank you!" cried Wilbur, as he soared and swooped from one end of the universe to the other—faster than the speed of light.

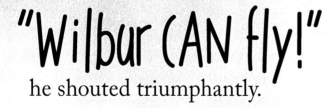

"Wilbur CAN fly!"

he shouted triumphantly.

And fly he did ... forever after.

About the Author

Deftly wielding his SwordPen, **Zev "Wilbur" Lewinson** has created a true classic with this latest literary work for children, *The Hippo That Flew*. It is Zev's second release by Sword-Pen Publishers.

A voracious reader, Zev and his "navigator" wife Sharen (yes, it was *love at first flight*) reside in New York, where they are being brought up by their five gorgeous hippos—ages 8 through 23—who all flash blank expressions when asked what their father does for a living. While it's hard to say what he does to support his family—or rather, what he hasn't done—luckily for his young readers, his passion is writing.

About the Illustrator

Once again, **Debi Coules** has waved her magical brushes to create an incredible work of art in *The Hippo That Flew*. With more styles than you'll find in any art history book, Debi has combined her incredible imagination and skilled SwordBrush to illustrate a true classic.

Debi's background in art has been seen in fashion designs and covers for *Newsweek* magazine. Good thing for us that her favorite form of artistic expression is illustrating children's stories. Debi lives in Philadelphia with her husband Michael. Their home is a bit emptier since Matthew left for college. Fortunately, Debi still has the loyal devotion of her "daughter" Samilla, a beautiful yellow Labrador retriever.

add
& elaborate on

Wilbur's childhood
Young adulthood
old age

Stop being Willie Loman, this is if earned. We have bills to
pay & children & raise. Come out of the garage. Stop your
tinkering in there.

Never gives up.   Determined

Willbur
Will "power" bur

Nevertheless, Wilbur dies with his dream unfulfilled & goes to
heaven. He is eulogized sadly as a child that lived in fantasy,
was beloved by children, but never got to see his life dream fulfilled.

② Why, asked Wilbur, it never succeeded in my quest for flight.

③ Incredible rewards await you Wilbur said the Voice.

④ The ability to fly always was there in your mind. You
did not live long enough to figure out the nuts & the
bolts, the details. "Don't worry about that now," The
Voice said, as a flash of light suddenly entered Wilbur. Instantly
Wilbur felt happy beyond description.
"You now have the ability to fly faster than the speed of light,"
The Voice said. "You can also hover, take off vertically,
horizontally. Your flight will only be limited by your
imagination." "Thank You," cried Wilbur. "Thank You"
Thank You! *" One little last detail," said the Voice firmly.
"Yes," said Wilbur hesitatingly. The Voice replied lovingly,
"This gift is yours for eternity!"

The Beginning

* as he instantly soared from
one end of the universe to the other

Name (print)	Exp. Date	Time In	Time Out	Signature
20.				
19.				
18.				
17.				
16.				
15.				
14.				
13.				
12.				
11.				
10.				
9.				
8.				
7.				
6.				
5.				
4.				
3.				
2.				
1.				

③ "Ah! But you did succeed Wilbur. You are an inspiration to all those who live on Earth after you. You held onto your belief, inspite of anything uncovered to told onto! You believed in yourself, and individuals that are just now being born will pick up your notebooks + continue your work + your vision. Flight will happen for mankind Wilbur. And it will happen because of you!", said The Voice.

Attendant on Duty _____ Date _____

SwordPen Publishers is the quality book publisher that has children's best interests at heart. Our deep commitment to nurturing the *joys of reading* early in life is the guiding principle behind our gentle, engaging stories, and is expressed by our mission to create true *literature for young readers*.

SwordPen's books are educational and informative while also being entertaining. Each volume is crafted and created to become a family heirloom that today's children will one day read to their own.

Look for the SwordPen imprint and ensconce your children with a priceless library of books that they will cherish—books about which they will surely proclaim, *"It's my favorite story!"*

SwordPen Publishers cares about every word your child reads. On that you have Our Word.

1(866)Our-Word

Interested in checking out more great stories for kids? Visit our gallery at **www.swordpen.com** to view present and future heirlooms.